STEVE BARLOW ✝ STEVE SKIDMORE

DEMON
HUNTER

iHorror
now available...

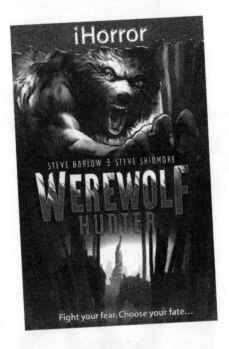

iHorror

DEMON
HUNTER

Steve Barlow
&
Steve Skidmore

Illustrated by
Paul Davidson

ORCHARD BOOKS

ORCHARD BOOKS
338 Euston Road, London NW1 3BH
Orchard Books Australia
Level 17/207 Kent St, Sydney, NSW 2000

A Paperback Original
First published in Great Britain in 2011

A CIP catalogue record for this book is available from
the British Library.

ISBN 978 1 40830 988 9

1 3 5 7 9 10 8 6 4 2

Printed in Great Britain

The paper and board used in this paperback are natural recyclable
products made from wood grown in sustainable forests. The
manufacturing processes conform to the environmental regulations of
the country of origin.

Orchard Books is a division of Hachette Children's Books,
an Hachette UK company

www.hachette.co.uk

iHorror

"*You better watch out,
unless you want to die.*"

Victoria Boatwright

iHorror

There is a dark, unseen world around us, of
supernatural horrors beyond our imagination.
Sometimes the worlds of humans and horrors
collide, threatening our very existence.

In iHorror, you make decisions that will affect
how the story unfolds. Each section of this book is
numbered. At the end of most sections, you will have
to make a choice. The choice you make will take you
to a different section of the book.

Some of your choices will help you to complete the
adventure successfully. But choose wisely. Make the
wrong choice and you could wind up dead!

Dare you enter the world of iHorror?
Fight your fear. Choose your fate...

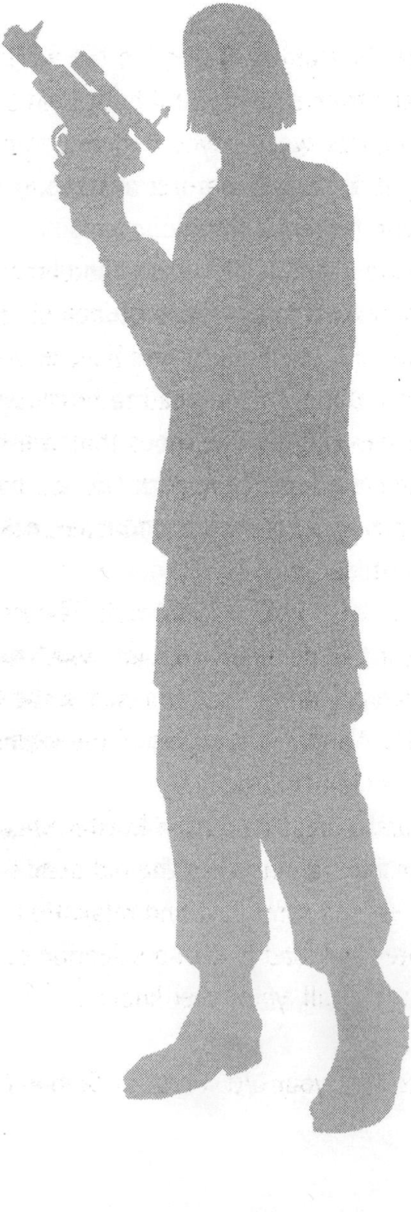

Who is the Hunter?

You are the Hunter, protecting the world of humans from supernatural horrors in all their forms. Vampires, werewolves, demons, zombies – you have fought all these creatures and more, and you've always beaten them... so far.

Over more years than you can remember you have become an expert in martial arts, including Jujitsu, Wing Chun and Taekwondo, and have amassed a store of weapons. But even you need to brush up on these skills and seek out new weapons that will help you to defeat the creatures of the dark. So, you have come to Japan to meet your instructor, Master Shoki, a retired demon hunter.

Although he is now old and frail, Master Shoki is an expert in the demons of Japan, which are some of the strangest and most ferocious in the world. Fortunately, they are creatures of the underworld – trapped beneath the earth.

You learn a great deal from Master Shoki. After your intensive training with the old demon hunter, you have earned some rest and relaxation. You hire a helicopter and load it with a selection of new weapons: after all, you never know...

Prepare to face your latest test in *Demon Hunter*.

And so it begins...

You fly to the southern Japanese island of Okinawa, and land your helicopter on a hilltop overlooking an open-air sumo stadium. You stroll down into the stadium to watch the sumo wrestling championships.

Two sumo wrestlers, wearing nothing but their *mawashi* fighting belts, are preparing to fight. They throw handfuls of salt across the ring and go into a ritual warm-up, raising their legs in the air and stamping down again with great force.

Suddenly, there is a deafening rumble from beneath the earth, and the ground shakes. The wrestlers look at each other with puzzled expressions. You are immediately on your guard – even two sumo giants can't be heavy enough to cause an earthquake, you think. For a moment there is silence. Then, over the hill behind the stadium, dark clouds gather. Strange lights flash among the seething vapours, and ear-splitting, unearthly cries fill the air.

You look up towards the gathering clouds and realise that something very bad is happening...

‡ *Go to 1.*

1

Suddenly two new wrestlers appear from the hill. They are gigantic: their bodies are bright red, and they have savage expressions with staring eyes, bulbous noses and wide mouths filled with gnashing teeth. One has arms so long that it has to carry them high above its head to avoid tripping over them. The other has tiny arms, but incredibly long legs.

You know that these are not human wrestlers: they are demons. The earthquake that shook the ground must have opened a portal to the underworld, allowing them to escape.

There is complete panic in the stadium as the demon wrestlers leap into the ring. Long-arms hurls the terrified sumo competitors high into the air, and Long-legs stamps around the ring, taunting and jeering at the fleeing audience.

You need to act quickly and decisively, but you have left your weapons in the helicopter. What should you do?

‡ *To head up the hill to get some weapons from the helicopter, go to 64.*

‡ *To use your martial arts skills to attack the demons, go to 30.*

‡ *If you want to think more carefully about what you should do, go to 73.*

2

You take a cola from the SUV's built-in fridge and crack the tab to open it. You lean against the car and drink, savouring the feel of the cool liquid on your parched throat.

But the ground shudders again. Another earthquake, or an aftershock of the first, has struck the city! The island rocks and huge cracks appear in the ground. One opens directly below the SUV, which begins to sink. Frantically, you climb into the car, start the engine and put the vehicle in gear: but the wheels spin uselessly. You dive out of the sinking car and scrabble for the edge of the split in the earth: but before you can escape, scores of demons rise out of the newly created pit, surrounding you.

You watch as the car with all your weapons falls into the gaping pit. You face the demons, defenceless.

‡   *Go to 55.*

3

You load your weapons into a backpack and run to the nearest Metro station. You take the escalator down to the platform.

The station is deserted: you guess that most people have heard about the demon invasion and are staying out of harm's way.

Luckily the trains seem to be running. The rails begin to hum, a destination signboard flashes, and you see lights approaching from the tunnel.

At the same time, you hear wails and gibbering voices coming from the platform exits. Shadows appear, advancing upon you. The platform lights begin to go out one at a time. You realise that the station is not as deserted as it appears to be, and brace yourself to meet the attack of whatever demons have found their way down here. As the platform is plunged into darkness, you pull out your gun and put on your night-vision goggles. You see nothing, but your Hunter instincts tell you that there are demons about.

At that moment, the train pulls in and the doors hiss open. You back into the carriage, watching the platform, carefully. After a moment, the doors close and you start to relax.

You hear a noise and quickly turn your head. Your blood turns cold – the carriage is full of demons!

They hurl themselves at you, snapping at your body with their razor-sharp teeth; ripping into your soft flesh. The train sets off slowly – but you will never reach its destination. For you, the next stop is death...

‡ *Your hunt is over. If you wish to begin again, go to 1.*

4

In a flash, you load your shotgun with rock-salt cartridges. As the demon head bounces towards you, you aim the weapon and blaze away.

But your shots have no effect against the tough, stone head.

You will have to change tactics!

- ‡ *To shoot the head with dragon's breath cartridges, go to 37.*
- ‡ *To attack the demon head with your sword, go to 56.*
- ‡ *If you wish to head back for more weapons, go to 93.*

5

There are screams from the people below as they see the child falling towards the ground. You can hear people cursing you for your lack of humanity.

You look up – the hibagon stands on the wheel crying out and beating its chest. The air is immediately full of the sound of beating wings as hundreds of demons answer their master's call and fly towards the Ferris wheel.

The demons launch their attack, smothering you and snapping at your body with their sharp, malevolent teeth. Your weapons are ripped from you as more and more demons attack, shredding your clothes and skin. Blood spurts out from your wounds.

You try to hang on desperately, but it is no use. The demons slash and rip at your hands. Slowly, but surely, finger-by-finger you lose your grip. You fall backwards and plummet downwards, just like the child you didn't try to save. In seconds, you smash into the ground, where more demons rip and tear at your broken body, before you thankfully pass into blackness.

‡ *If you wish to begin again, go to 1.*

5: Hundreds of winged demons attack you.

6

The undead demons swarm all over you, holding you helpless in their foul clutches. Their rotting flesh seeps revolting fluids, which drip onto your cringing body; the stench of their breath makes you gag. You struggle, but the demons' grip is too strong.

The nukekubi stoops over you and breathes in, sucking all the life from your body. You feel your flesh decay and putrefy. Your lips pull back from your rotting teeth; your skin shrivels, your bones crumble. As the final seconds of your life pass, you wonder whether a demon will inhabit your festering corpse to turn you, too, into a goryo zombie.

‡ *Your hunt is over. If you wish to begin again, go to 1.*

7

You raise your bow and shoot the shikome with arrows. Many are destroyed by the deadly ash-wood shafts, but more keep arriving. The horde of demons seems never-ending and some of their attacks are getting through. Their talons rip into your flesh.

‡ *If you choose to continue to fight here, go to 97.*
‡ *To seek shelter in the temple, go to 22.*
‡ *To head for the cliff and climb to the hilltop, go to 29.*

8

You pick up the stars and race towards the Ferris wheel, where the demon horde is causing mayhem. But suddenly, you stagger back as if you have run into a brick wall. You look around, but see nothing. Then a punch lifts you off your feet. You sprawl on the ground and quickly realise you are fighting an invisible demon!

You stagger to your feet, lift your shotgun and fire from the hip. Your shots have no effect. You are shooting empty air! Another blow sends you flying.

You pick yourself up off the ground. "So you want to play hide-and-seek?" you mutter. "Okay, you're 'it'!"

You raise the shotgun again, but this time you quickly change ammunition and fire a series of dragon's breath cartridges. There is a scream, and you can see the outline of the invisible demon ringed in flame. You skim a throwing star at it: the star is a magic pentagram. The demon outline vanishes as its unearthly body is trapped inside the five-pointed star.

But more demons are approaching, in all shapes and sizes. You switch ammunition to the rock-salt cartridges and destroy a few of them, but there are more. You throw more stars and trap other demons, but you are running out of ammunition!

‡ *To use your hand-to-hand fighting skills, go to 30.*
‡ *To return to the SUV to get more weapons, go to 76.*

9

You lower your head in a bow. Hashuk is a goddess: even if you did not need her help, it would be unwise to offend her. "Thank you, Hashuk-san. Your fame as a hunter of demons is legendary. I would be honoured if you would hunt with me."

Hashuk laughs. "You have good manners, mortal."

You indicate the motorbike's pillion seat. "Will you ride with me?"

Hashuk's eyes flash. "Hashuk has no need of the devices of men. Ride your stinking machine if you must: for the way is long. I shall run."

The bird on her shoulder gives a harsh cry and takes flight. Hashuk sets off after it, running like the wind. You follow her on the motorbike, bouncing and skidding over the rough track.

At last, the forest gives way to a grassy slope. You have reached the foothills of the sacred mountain: Mount Fuji. But your way is blocked. Two gigantic demons stand on the slope above you – one in the shape of a huge, savage dog, and the other made of shards and spears of frozen water – an icicle demon.

Hashuk laughs. "Time to prove your worth, Hunter."

‡ *If you decide to attack the dog demon, go to 96.*
‡ *If you choose to fight the icicle demon, go to 27.*

10

You head through the broken gates into the zoo.

You prowl along pathways scattered with debris, past wrecked enclosures torn apart by the demon-possessed creatures seeking their freedom.

A snuffling noise stops you in your tracks. Emerging from the wreck of a refreshment kiosk, licking at the contents on a five-litre carton of ice cream, is an enormous demon bear. It spots you and gives a ferocious snarl.

The bear hurls itself towards you, its slavering jaws open and deadly claws ready to strike you dead.

‡ *If you want to shoot it with rock salt, go to 48.*
‡ *If you choose to use the hanbo staff, go to 71.*

11

You raise your shotgun and fire at the hibagon. But the shotgun is not an accurate weapon from this distance. You miss the demon and hit the child's leg instead. It cries out in pain.

The child's parents scream with horror and despair. Appalled by what you have done, you stare upwards, stunned. You drop your weapons in sheer horror.

This gives your enemies the chance they need. Two small blue-coloured demons rush in and gather up your weapons. When you come to your senses, you realise that you are surrounded by demons.

‡ *To try to get your weapons in the SUV, go to 76.*
‡ *If you wish to take the demons on using your martial arts skills, go to 30.*

12

You begin to climb the wheel. The demons that have been swarming over it slither to attack. You raise your shotgun and fire single-handed, destroying several demons. The others pull back, hissing and spitting with frustration. More demons cluster at the base of the Ferris wheel, baying for your blood.

You follow the hibagon up the metal frame of the wheel. Your muscles ache with the exertion, but you know you have to rescue the child. The creature is within the range of your gun, but you daren't risk shooting and hitting the child.

The hibagon reaches the top of the stationary wheel and turns to jeer at you. Gloating, it drops the child. Far below, its mother screams.

‡ *To try to save the child, go to 20.*
‡ *If you decide you cannot help the child and should attack the hibagon, go to 5.*

13

You grit your teeth and press your foot down hard on the accelerator. You hit the waterspout. Spray lashes around the car, which slips and slides as the roadway tilts and tips. But the waterspout has washed away some of the cars that were blocking your progress off the bridge, and sent fleeing pedestrians scurrying for shelter: so that when you eventually break through the waterspout, the way ahead is clear...

But not for long. Water demons flood across the roadway and more climb the parapet to join them. You do not hesitate. "Gangway!" you cry. "Hunter coming through!"

You keep the pedal to the metal, and your speed takes you through the demons, hurling many aside as the rest scatter.

You have almost broken clear when a kappa, the most agile of the demons, jumps onto the bonnet of the car, blocking your view.

‡ *If you want to brake suddenly, go to 17.*
‡ *If you want to open the window and drag the kappa out of the way, go to 43.*
‡ *If you want to get out of the car and fight the demons, go to 63.*

14

You slash at the nukekubi's head with the sickle and succeed in keeping it off. It circles around and attacks again – this time, you score a lucky hit, gouging out one of the creature's eyeballs. The demon roars with pain and anger.

But while you have been distracted by the demon's head, you have forgotten about the rest of its body. The creature's headless body grabs you from behind in a vice-like grip. You drop your weapon and it goes spinning off the roof and disappears from view.

As you try to break free, the nukekubi's head flies to its shoulders and reattaches. Seeing you helpless, the rest of the demons surge forward and you are overwhelmed.

‡ *Go to 6.*

15

You drag the woman away from the man and shoot a rock-salt cartridge into his body at point-blank range. He falls to the ground, screaming. The woman collapses into your arms.

But you suddenly realise that something isn't right. The man is still screaming and he is bleeding. His body isn't dissolving into the air, as a demon's would. To your horror, you realise that you have shot an innocent man! You look down at the woman in your arms – just as her face contorts into a savage mask. She is not human – she is a demon, and when you snatched her away from the big man – her intended victim – she turned her attention to you!

Horrified, you try to break away. But the demon woman has a grip of iron. Her skin ripples as her face loses any kind of humanity. Her dress flows as though it is alive: where it touches you, your skin burns as though dipped in acid. She tightens her grasp, and laughs as, screaming horribly, you feel your skin dissolve and your bones liquefy as the demon absorbs your body into her own unearthly substance.

‡ *Your hunt is over. If you are brave enough to try again, go to 1.*

16

You slip out from the back of the temple and climb the mountain, the shi-shi running at your side.

But soon, thick mist descends. As you run on, you realise that you are surrounded by demon shapes. These are the dreaded tengu, demons taking the monstrous forms of dogs, hawks and humans with grotesque, swollen noses who control the forces of nature.

A man-shaped demon flings out its hand, and one of your shi-shi allies is blown from the mountainside by a howling wind. A hawk-shaped tengu flaps its wings, and your other companion is vaporised by a lightning bolt. You curse helplessly – the shi-shi though willing, were not powerful enough to meet the challenge. As you continue your climb, wind howls around you, thunder deafens you and lightning scorches the rocks at your feet. It is as though you were being herded up the mountain by the storm.

And now, as you approach the crater of Mount Fuji, you look up into the pitiless eyes of the greatest and most terrifying demon of all – Shinigami, Lord of Death.

‡ *Go to 80.*

17

"Okay, big-mouth," you say, "time to get off."

You slam on the brakes. The kappa loses its grip and flies off the bonnet. You immediately floor the accelerator again. The tyres screech and then there is a horrible wet splat from beneath the wheels as you run over your former passenger. "That's what I call toad-kill," you mutter grimly.

The demons ahead of you explode into nothingness and you realise that the kappa must have been chief demon of the water-creatures. You have destroyed another nest of the demon invaders!

But with the Rainbow Bridge destroyed, you have to find an alternative route to reach Master Shoki. The streets of Tokyo are full of abandoned cars – you have to weave between them, shoving some out of the way.

At last you reach Master Shoki and make your report. "You have done well, Hunter-san," he tells you. "But the last aftershock released more demons."

"I know, but I've got rid of the water demons."

"No, there are more. There is a horde of demons at Ueno zoo. You will have to defeat them. Time is running out – go quickly."

The roads are jammed. How will you get to the zoo?

‡ *If you decide to use the helicopter, go to 34.*
‡ *If you want to use the Metro, go to 3.*

18

You stumble through the evil-smelling ooze and catch up with the huntress. "Hashuk, what's wrong? Why don't you answer me?"

She turns and brushes the hair from her face. It's savage and evil, with blood-red eyes and needle-sharp teeth. You remember one of Master Shoki's lessons too late. "Some gods and goddesses hate demons as much as humans do, Hunter-san, and may come to your aid. But beware! Demons also know this. For example, Kanesh, a blood-sucking monster, imitates Hashuk the Huntress to lure people into her trap..."

The demon Kanesh attacks. You fight her off with your tonfa club. She steps back and shoots an arrow – you try to dodge, but the shaft passes through your thigh. You cry out with pain and fall to the ground.

The demon leaps in for the kill. You snatch an arrow from your quiver, but you have no time to shoot it: instead, you thrust it forward. The ash-wood shaft stabs into Kanesh's body and through her heart. With a scream of agony, she dissolves into dust.

You pick up a large stick and use it as a crutch. You stumble through the forest, but you are weak from loss of blood, and your wounded leg slows you down.

At length you emerge from the forest.

‡ *Go to 86.*

19

You dance around the edge of the ring, taunting and shouting at the demons, trying to separate them.

Growling, Long-arms reaches for you. You dance out of the demon's way. Long-legs aims a kick at you. You dodge this, and continue to weave about the sumo ring, shouting insults.

But these demons, though savage, are not stupid. They seem to guess what you are trying to do. Neither will leave the other to chase you. Your strategy is not working, and every passing second makes it more likely that you will provoke the ashin into joining together and becoming ten times more powerful than before. What should you do now?

  ‡ *If you want to attack the demons using your martial arts skills, go to 30.*
  ‡ *If you wish to head for the helicopter to get your weapons, go to 64.*

20

Your reaction is instinctive – you wrap your legs around a girder, and reach out with your arms. For a moment you think you are not going to make it, but you reach out further and pluck the child from the air.

The little girl clings to you, sobbing with fright, as

you edge out along the girder and put her in one of the Ferris wheel's passenger cars.

"Stay there," you tell her, "you'll be safe for the moment." Then you start climbing again. You have unfinished business with the hibagon.

You reach the top of the wheel and face the demon. The hibagon roars and swipes at you with claws like butchers' cleavers.

You dance out of reach. "Too slow, furball." In one fluid movement, you draw your katana sword and thrust it towards the gigantic creature's chest. The blade passes through the demon's body and the magical kanji inscribed on its blade act immediately. The demon howls and explodes in a cloud of dust.

You watch the remains of the hibagon drift away on the wind. "Well, look at that," you say. "Hiba-gone."

Instantly, all the demons on the wheel and those gathered below dissolve into nothingness. You have destroyed the master demon of this nest, and condemned the others to oblivion.

You return the child to its relieved parents and head back to the SUV.

‡ *If you decide that the threat is over and you can relax, go to 2.*

‡ *If you think you should return to Master Shoki and find out what else is happening, go to 75.*

21

You race to the scene of the demon attack. Grotesque monsters crawl all over the Ferris wheel, giggling and launching lightning bolts at the crowds below.

Your way is blocked by a creature that seems to be wearing a long, black cloak. You then realise that the cloak is part of its body! This creature doesn't look too dangerous, so you attempt to sidestep it.

Suddenly, the cloak swirls around you. Everything goes dark and you realise that you cannot breathe: you are suffocating in the folds of the strange cloak.

You lash out with the deer-horn knife. Great rips appear in the cloak, and air rushes in. You fill your lungs and continue to shred the cloak. The demon wails and turns to run: you load a rock-salt cartridge into the shotgun and blast it apart.

But more demons are approaching. One knife is not going to be enough! You raise the shotgun again, but this time you fire a series of dragon's breath cartridges. Several demons are scorched and disappear in a mass of flame and smoke. You switch back to rock-salt cartridges and blow some more demons to pieces, but there are still more coming. Soon you realise that you are running out of ammunition.

‡ *To use your hand-to-hand fighting skills, go to 30.*
‡ *To get more ammunition from the SUV, go to 76.*

22

You run through the gateway leading to the temple. The demons pour after you – but at the gate they stop, howling with frustration. They dare not enter the sacred precincts. They snarl at you, spitting and cursing and howling threats of what they will do to you if they catch you.

"You demons really do have anger management issues," you smile. "Adios, boys and girls."

You run on, up the processional way flanked by stone toro lanterns, until you arrive at the temple itself. You bow as a mark of respect, but as you go to step between the two stone lions guarding the second gateway, they come to life and prowl towards you, growling a warning. These are shi-shi, the guardians of the holy place, and they are clearly not prepared to let you through unchallenged.

‡ *If you choose to attack the shi-shi, go to 32.*
‡ *If you decide to submit to them and ask for help, go to 90.*

23

You climb into the cockpit of the helicopter, take out your shotgun and load it. You hurry through the pre-flight checks, then start the engine and grip the

22: The stone lion guardians come to life.

controls tightly. The rotors bite the air above your head and you climb away from the ground, bursting through the smoke that surrounds the hilltop before heading towards the stadium.

You peer down and see the ashin demons causing havoc. Crowds of people are running from the stadium, trying to escape and screaming in total panic. You can also see bodies lying on the ground – it is hard to make out whether they are dead or just injured.

You have to make a decision – fast!

Should you land the helicopter and arm yourself with the weapons that are in the cargo hold, or fly over the demons and attack them from the air?

‡ *If you want to land, go to 85.*
‡ *If you want to fly the helicopter and shoot at the demons, go to 47.*

24

You fly the helicopter back to the office block. You manage to land just as the fuel gauge reads empty. You meet Master Shoki and tell him how you have fared in the battle against the Ueno Park demons.

Master Shoki's face is ashen. "I regret to say, Hunter-san, that the threat is not over."

You groan. "What else is out there?"

"Undead demons."

"Huh? I thought all demons were undead."

"Technically, yes. But these demons take the form of corpses – ogres – ghouls – hags..."

"All right," you say wearily, "where are they?"

"Somewhere between here and Kyoto. They have hijacked a Shinkasen..."

You stare at him. "A bullet train? How did they...?"

Master Shoki shakes his head impatiently. "There is no time to explain. You must stop them before they spread their infection to the rest of Japan."

"All right," you say. "But the helicopter is out of fuel and I won't be able to get more until all the excitement is over. How can I get to the train?"

"I've assembled the jet-kite," he says coolly.

"The one that's never been flown?" you say. "The one you said was purely experimental?"

"Correct." Master Shoki points to a assemblage of gleaming metal and brightly-coloured fabric.

The jet-kite would allow you to get to the train quickly, but should you put your trust in an untried piece of equipment? Or should you take a slower, but safer option?

‡ *To head for the station to catch the next bullet train, you will need to take the Metro. Go to 3.*

‡ *To take your SUV and pursue the train, go to 68.*

‡ *To take Master Shoki's jet-kite, go to 45.*

25

You turn the key and hit the starter – but nothing happens. You try again and again, with no result. You realise that the water washing over the bridge has got into the car's electrical system. The engine will not start, and the demons are getting closer.

You get out of the car. More and more demons are heading towards you, baring their teeth and emitting unearthly howls, causing you to shudder and your blood to turn cold. You have to make a snap decision.

‡ *To try to fight your way out of this mess, go to 63.*
‡ *If you decide to jump from the bridge and swim to safety, go to 95.*

26

Ignoring the pleading family, you load your shotgun with standard cartridges and blaze away at the wheel. Your shots bounce off without effect. You switch to rock salt with no better result.

You curse as you realise that the wheel is made of real iron and is not part of the demon itself. Rock salt will harm the demon – if you can hit it – but will have no effect on the wheel.

You switch your aim to the rider, but it is too late.

The demon leaps astride the wheel, its legs growing bigger before your eyes.

The savage creature's legs straddle the wheel, like the front forks of a bicycle, and it steers the fiery wheel towards you. You aim your gun at the demon, but you are too late. The blazing wheel knocks you down and runs over your legs, simultaneously roasting them and crushing them into the ground. You lie in helpless agony as the crazed demon turns the wheel. With an inhuman screech, it bears down on you again. You close your eyes in the knowledge that you are about to be crushed into a smoking pulp.

‡ *You have died trying to defeat the demons.*
If you are brave enough to begin again, go to 1.

27

You attack and grapple with the icicle demon, whilst Hashuk deals with the dog demon.

Your body is suddenly racked by a wave of intense cold. Your hands are instantly numb; you shiver uncontrollably.

You draw your tonfa club. You swing it with all your strength, but on contact with the demon, the club freezes and shatters. Before you can move, the demon reaches out and pulls you into its cold embrace. Icicles, as sharp as knives and spears, stab through your frozen body. You see the goddess shooting dead the dog demon, before shooting an arrow at the icicle demon. The creature shatters into thousands of shards. But this is too late for you.

‡ *You will not be able to save the world from the demons. If you wish to try again, go to 1.*

28

You rush to the attack, but the spider-woman is fast and agile. She climbs up out of reach on a silken line.

Unable to stop, you fall straight into her web that in your haste you failed to notice. Silk threads – sticky, thick and as strong as steel – cling to every part of you.

In desperation, you try to raise your gun – but you cannot. It is caught in the silk net along with your hanbo staff. You are helpless.

The spider cackles. "Come into my parlourrr, said the spiderrr to the fly..." Its mouth widens horribly, and a set of mandibles emerges, clicking and quivering. Venom drips from her poison fangs.

Then it pounces. The agony is intense but brief as the venom is injected into your helpless body: then numbness spreads through you as your bones, organs and muscles begin to rot and liquefy. Soon you will be merely a bag of swirling juices, and the demon spider will drink her fill.

‡ *Your hunt is over. If you want to begin again, turn to 1.*

29

You climb the cliff, but even an expert mountaineer like you cannot use weapons at the same time.

The shikome, cackling with glee and shrieking with delight, torment you, slashing at your unprotected head, shoulders and back with their dreadful claws. Their sharp talons continue to rip open your flesh and your shirt is soon soaked with your blood. In spite of the agony, you manage to hold on and climb further up the rock face. The attacks continue as you edge nearer and nearer to the top. The creatures seem to know that soon you will be able to use your weapons so they attack faster and harder. Their deadly talons rip further into your flesh and gouge at your eyes. You are helpless against the demons' savagery. You lose your grip, and fall to your death on the jagged rocks below.

‡ *You have failed and paid the ultimate price.*
If you want to begin again, go to 1.

30

The demons move towards you and emit ear-piercing screams. These unworldly sounds seem to be a signal and, to your horror, dozens more demons in a variety of grotesque shapes appear. Within seconds you are surrounded. You realise that you have no chance of defeating so many opponents. Escape is impossible.

They close in, slashing at your unprotected body. Your martial arts skills are no match for these creatures of the underworld. Your blood spurts in fountains as the demons tear you to pieces.

⚜ *If you wish to begin your adventure again, go to 1.*

31

"I'll take the gun," you say. Then you step off the roof. For several seconds, you are in free-fall. Then the wind lifts your kite. As you level out, you fire up the jet pack and you shoot forward. Master Shoki's jet kite works!

You speed over the city, and then out over the dark countryside. You find the silver ribbon of the Kyoto railway line: then, far ahead, you see the lights of the bullet train.

You increase speed. Soon you are racing alongside the train. The demons inside the carriages howl and shake their claws at you as you swoop over the train and land on the roof.

At first, you have to use the thrust of the jet pack to maintain your position. Then the train slows. The windows of the carriage below you are smashed, and a horde of undead demons swarm onto the roof of the carriage. They seem to be able to cling to any surface. Soon you are surrounded by goryo – zombie-like corpses reanimated by demons.

The speed of the train is incredible, but you manage to keep your balance as you ready your weapon. You open fire with the shotgun – but though the rounds blast chunks of undead flesh from the demons' bodies, this doesn't even slow them up. They simply keep on coming until you are overwhelmed.

⸸ *Go to 88.*

32

The shi-shi's growl is like the grinding of the stone from which they are made. "What is your business here, Hunter?"

You aim an arrow at the nearest lion-creature. "Stay back, demon!"

The shi-shi roars. "We are guardians, not demons!"

"Demons who guard temples are demons just the same." You shoot again and again. Wounded by your arrows, the shi-shi return to stone.

You slip out of the back of the temple and head up Mount Fuji. You are quickly enveloped in mist. Demon shapes loom all around you – mountain-haunting tengu demons in the shapes of gigantic hawks, huge dogs and monstrous humans with grotesque, swollen noses.

Then, a sudden storm descends. You are battered by wind, deafened by thunder and blinded by lightning bolts. Still you climb, through the snowfields, to the very top of the sacred mountain – and there, as you approach the crater, you look up in horror. Before you stands the most terrifying demon of all – Shinigami, Lord of Death.

‡ *Go to 80.*

33

You watch in horror as Shinigami scoops handfuls of molten rock and hurls it at the two dragons.

The great beasts are helpless against such an attack. They spit their own fireballs at the Lord of Death, but the demon gestures and the flames are extinguished as easily as a candle is snuffed out.

Before the dragons can get nearer, Shinigami hurls more fireballs. Ryu is hit and explodes into ashes.

Kirin flies off, mourning for its companion. The Lord of Death is too powerful even for the guardians of mankind. Shinigami turns his attention back to you.

There is nothing left for you to do, but to beg for mercy.

‡ *Go to 84.*

34

You carry your remaining weapons up to the roof and load them into the helicopter.

You take off and fly across the stricken city. Below you, panicking crowds are pursued by demons.

You land in Ueno Park. The normally bustling gardens are a scene of chaos. The zoo animals have broken out of their cages – but their animal bodies are possessed by demons. They have grown monstrous, savage and merciless. Their features are distorted, their eyes glitter with hate.

You bite your lip. "You guys are really wild tonight." You decide to take your shotgun and one more type of weapon.

‡ *To choose a pair of ninjato short swords, go to 59.*
‡ *To choose a long, ash hanbo quarterstaff, go to 10.*

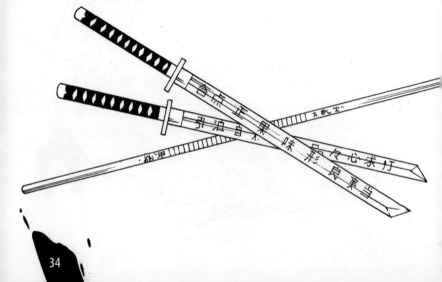

35

You rev the engine, turn your car round, recklessly slamming into empty cars and vans to shunt them out of the way, and head back along the bridge towards the safety of Odaiba Island.

But the road is blocked by abandoned vehicles. In between them, the people who have left their cars are running in panic to get away from the horror that has overtaken the bridge. Progress is slow. You glance in your rear-view mirror and see hundreds of demons crawling over the bridge.

A sound of roaring water causes you to jerk your head to the right. A great waterspout is rising from the bay. As the spout forms a funnel, towering above the bridge, the mocking face of a demon appears in the foaming water.

"That guy certainly knows how to make a splash," you mutter as the waterspout slams into the bridge in front of you, washing over the roadway.

‡ *If you choose to keep going and try to outrun it, go to 13.*
‡ *If you decide to stop and wait for the danger to subside, go to 87.*

36

"I do not trust demons," you say, "even those that offer help."

Hashuk's eyes glimmer like stars. "I am no demon, mortal! I hunt demons. I am a goddess."

You shrug. "Whatever you are, you are not human. I do not need your help."

"So be it." Hashuk turns and runs into the forest.

You kick the motorbike back into life and set off again. But soon, you realise that you are lost. All the forest tracks look the same, and the trees are so thick and tall that you can no longer see Mount Fuji. You lose your sense of direction, and regret not having listened to Hashuk.

You stop the motorbike and get off. You scramble up a mound to higher ground, where you can see Mount Fuji – but it is far in the distance. You know you will never reach the mountain in time.

‡ Go to 86.

37

You quickly load your gun with dragon's breath cartridges and shoot. The flaming tongue of the dragon's breath engulfs the demon head. Where its fire touches the surface, the stone blackens, then turns red, and finally splits. While the demon howls with rage and pain, you hurriedly switch ammunition, loading rock-salt cartridges, which you fire into the gaping wound.

Your plan works. By cracking the stone, you have managed to get at the deadly substance inside the demon, instead of the rounds bouncing off the head's tough exterior. The creature bounces around in agony, the stone head swelling and cracking – until eventually it explodes like a grenade, leaving nothing behind but a small cloud of smoke and ashes.

"Another one bites the dust," you mutter.

You turn back towards the Ferris wheel. The hibagon still has the child in its grasp and the demon wheel rider is causing mayhem.

⸭ *If you want to attack the hibagon, go to 81.*
⸭ *If you want to attack the demon wheel rider, go to 26.*

38

You pick up the mankiri and swing it around your head, before throwing it at your demon opponent, aiming for its legs. The chain hits the charging Long-legs just below the knees, exactly as you intended. The weights on the end of the chain wrap around the loathsome creature's calves, making it impossible for it to run. Long-legs topples forward with a roar and its head crashes against the hard ground.

You smile. But the mankiri is wrapped around Long-legs and even if you could recover it for a second throw, it would be no use against Long-arms. The vengeful demon, enraged at seeing its companion fall, gives a blood-curdling roar and seizes you. You cry out in pain as the demon rips your right arm from its socket. Blood spurts everywhere. You howl, as with agonising slowness, the dreadful creature tears you limb from limb.

‡ *If you are brave enough to begin your adventure again, go to 1.*

39

The head flies in for another attack, but you ignore it and shoot the nukekubi's body with an arrow.

The ash wood acts immediately. The kanji symbols glow bright and the demon's body stiffens: then it topples sideways and is swept along the roof of the train, sweeping ghouls, hags, goryo and other undead creatures off their feet to fall, wailing, from the train.

With a screech of rage, the head attacks again. You leap like a goalkeeper, and catch it in both hands.

"Currrse you, Hunterrr," the head snarls. "You think you have beaten us – but you are wrong." The demon cackles madly. "So wrong!"

‡ *If you want to listen to what the head has to say, go to 50.*
‡ *If you want to destroy the head immediately, go to 62.*

40

You hurl yourself into the attack. The baboons scatter. They are too fast for you. They surround you, just out of reach, taunting you. One throws a chokin vase decorated with a picture of Mount Fuji at you: it shatters against your skull. The others bounce up and down, screeching with glee.

"Ouch! That's it," you growl. "No more games."

There are too many to shoot, so you use the hanbo staff. You hurl yourself at the baboons, swinging the quarterstaff. You strike some and the kanji symbols glow red on their bodies. Several demons leave their victims: the freed baboons run away.

But there are too many demon baboons coming from too many directions for you to fight them all.

Suddenly, demons in all shapes and sizes join the fight. You curse as you realise that the baboons were

just a distraction for the other demons to group
together and attack you.

You swing your staff, but it is torn from your grip.
You revert to your shotgun and manage to get off a
few shots, but then that is ripped from your hands.
You are at their mercy.

‡ *Go to 30.*

41

You raise your bow and shoot. The ash-wood arrow
buries itself in a segment of the centipede, which
dissolves into dust. But the remaining parts of the
centipede instantly rejoin, leaving the creature almost
as powerful as before.

You realise that the centipede is not one demon,
but a colony of demons working together – each is a
segment of the centipede, and a centipede has a lot
of segments!

You shoot more arrows, but the shikome and the
remaining segments of the centipede renew their
attack: and now more demons emerge from the rocks
at the base of the cliff. You are in a tight spot!

‡ *If you decide to seek shelter in the temple, go to 22.*
‡ *If you wish to continue the fight, go to 97.*

42

You turn and clamber frantically up the slopes of the pit, pursued by howling demons.

But you are exhausted. You fall to your knees: the palms of your hands are cut to ribbons by the sharp stones and ashes that form the sides of the pit.

The earth shudders again. You realise to your horror that the pit is closing. If you fall back, you will be caught by the demons, and carried off into their underground hell to endure a world of torment.

You struggle on, but the walls of the pit continue to close in. You realise you are not going to make it. You give a final scream of agony as the rift closes, covering your body as a thousand tons of rock crush you to an agonising death.

⚷ *Your hunt is over. If you wish to begin again, go to 1.*

43

You reach out, grab the kappa by its wrinkly shoulder. But the creature snatches your arm and heaves you halfway out of the car. You try to break free, but the demon laughs as you then lose control of the SUV. It smashes into a bridge support. The car explodes in a fireball, spins through the barrier, and plunges off the road like a flaming comet into the dark water below.

> ‡ *Your hunt is over. If you want to begin again, go to 1.*

44

You raise the shotgun and pull the trigger. The weapon jerks in your hand as you fire rock-salt ammunition into the demon. The salt rips through the ghastly creature, causing it to writhe and scream as the demonic forces that give its body life and substance are torn asunder.

Blazing lights spread from the wounds, as though a fire burns inside it. Finally, the creature explodes into dust and ashes, which are blown away on the wind.

You look up and see more demons preparing themselves for an attack.

> ‡ *If you think you need to get more weapons, go to 76.*
> ‡ *To carry on fighting the demons, go to 89.*

45

You strap on the jet-kite – a large delta wing with a jet pack. "This had better work," you mutter.

"If it does not," says Master Shoki, "I shall regret it very much."

"Not as much as I will!"

He gives you a bleak smile. "And weapons?"

"I'll take the tonfa and the kama."

Shoki hands you the tonfa – a baton with a side handle that acts as a combination armshield and club, and a kama folding sickle. You strap them on.

Master Shoki checks your equipment. "I calculate you can carry one more weapon." He holds out the shotgun. "Will you take this?"

"I used up all the special anti-demon ammo," you tell him. "I don't suppose you have any more?"

Master Shoki shakes his head. "Only conventional ammunition. Or there is the yumi longbow." He holds out the bow and a quiver full of ash-wood arrows. "Which will you choose?"

‡ *If you wish to choose the yumi bow, go to 99.*
‡ *If you wish to choose the shotgun, go to 31.*

46

"Thank you," you call, "but I will hunt alone now. Where is your bird? Ah! But you're not Hashuk! You're the demon Kanesh taking her form."

The demon throws her hair back, revealing blood-red eyes and a cruel mouth filled with razor-sharp teeth. "You are right... But now I am the hunter and you are the hunted!" She lunges to attack you.

But even before you can react, Hashuk leaps between you and her evil double. Kanesh snarls.

Hashuk calls over her shoulder, "Go on to the mountain, Hunter, I shall deal with this imposter!"

Screaming with rage, the Huntress and demon battle together: but you must continue your journey to the mountain.

‡ *Go to 61.*

47

You fly the helicopter towards the demons, slide open the side door and loose off a couple of shots. However, flying the helicopter and trying to take aim at the same time, proves too difficult. The shots have no impact, and now the demons have spotted you.

The ashin take immediate action. Long-arms picks up Long-legs and flings him upwards at incredible

46: Hashuk battles with her demon double.

speed, heading straight for you. You try to swerve away, but it is too late. Long-legs aims a kick at the helicopter. His gigantic foot smashes the machine in two, sending you plummeting towards the rocky hillside like a stone.

‡ *Your hunt is over. If you wish to begin again, go to 1.*

48

The shotgun blast is effective! The controlling demon screams as the rock salt enters the bear's flesh, and leaves its victim. The bear looks startled for a moment as its features lose their crazed ferocity and it shrinks to its normal size. Then, with a sigh, it falls down dead.

You feel no triumph – only remorse that you have destroyed such a beautiful creature. But what's done is done. There are still plenty of demons causing havoc. A bloated spider with a woman's face is hanging from a nearby tree, a troop of demon baboons is trashing a souvenir shop – and an orochi, an eight-headed dragon, is heading out of the park intent on causing yet more chaos.

‡ *To tackle the spider-woman, go to 28.*
‡ *To attack the baboons, go to 40.*
‡ *To tackle the orochi, go to 83.*

49

You jump into the river. The cold of the water takes your breath away, but you swim on.

The shikome make no attempt to attack you: the demons are clearly afraid of the water. The shikome scream angrily at you, before one of the bolder ones attacks. You reach up and grab its scrawny, scaly legs: it screeches and beats at you with its wings, but you hang on and pull it into the river to drown...

Suddenly you realise why the shikome are holding back. You remember about your earlier encounter with water demons. Now you realise that they are here, too. You are suddenly surrounded by frog-like kappa. As you swim to escape, you cannot stop them stealing your remaining weapons.

By the time you haul yourself out onto the islet, you are exhausted and unable to resist as a horde of demons surrounds you.

You take on some of them, using your martial arts skills, but no amount of kicking and punching will drive the hordes of demons back. They drive you to the centre of the island and to the smoking pit, concealed by the surrounding trees, from which they have emerged.

‡ *Go to 55.*

50

The nukekubi's head chortles with triumph and spite. "Foolish mortal! While you have been playing the hero, the greatest demons in all Japan have awakened. They are making their way to Mount Fuji."

You cannot hide your shock at this news. "Why?"

"To wake the volcano!" screams the head. "To stir the fires beneath the earth and to release the greatest demon of all: Shinigami, Lord of Death!"

The head bursts into gales of demonic laughter. Rage surges through your body, and you bury the sickle blade in the nukekubi's head. Its laughter ceases. At the same moment, all the undead demons of its nest vanish into nothingness.

You must get to Mount Fuji! You find the power car and stop the train. You jog away from the tracks. After a few minutes, you find yourself in a village. A motorcycle is lying in the road, the keys still in the ignition. You kick-start the machine to life, and head for the distant, snow-capped peak of Mount Fuji.

You leave the farmland and enter a forest. As you ride along a track, you become aware of a human figure running through the trees alongside you, at a greater speed than any mortal could manage.

You lose sight of the figure – but as you round a bend, a long-legged female figure appears in the headlights. You brake, and slide to a halt.

The woman has long dark hair. She carries a bow, with an arrow notched to the string. A hawk sits on her shoulder, glaring at you.

"I am Hashuk," she says. "Will you hunt with me?"

You remember Master Shoki once telling you about a Goddess called Hashuk, but what should you do?

‡ *If you decide to accept Hashuk's offer, go to 9.*
‡ *If you distrust her and want to decline, go to 36.*

51

You pick up the katana long sword and rush towards the Ferris wheel, which rears up out of a bank of unearthly mist. Demons swarm all over the vast structure, launching fireballs at the panicking crowds.

You fight your way through the stampede. A woman appears before you. She is beautiful, with long dark hair, and looks terrified. As you struggle towards her she bumps into a big, ugly-looking man. They become entangled in each other's arms. She looks up into his face, opens her mouth wide and gives an unearthly scream. You see some of the other demons looking at her before they turn away, as if they were frightened.

‡ *If you decide to shoot the man, go to 15.*
‡ *If you are suspicious about the situation,*
  go to 98.

52

You lash out with the tonfa. The club breaks undead bones and rips off chunks of undead flesh.

But the tonfa is a short-range weapon, for use at close quarters. Even as you dismember the demons in front of you, those behind you pounce. They smash into you and you fall to the roof of the train as they tear your weapons off. You spring to your feet, and lash out with your hands and feet. However, your martial arts skills are little use against these supernatural creatures of the dark.

✢ *Go to 88.*

53

You aim the gun and fire. The rock-salt cartridges blast one of the orochi's heads into bloody ribbons.

But the creature has seven more heads, and now it is angry. It roars with pain and lumbers after you.

As you run, you check the ammunition clip. Your stomach turns as you realise that whilst fighting the demons, you have used up most of your ammunition. You only have five more rock-salt cartridges. You know that the heads are the only vulnerable parts of the orochi. Even if you don't miss with a single shot, you will run out of ammunition before your opponent runs out of heads! And now more demons are appearing from all directions to join in the fight.

✢ *If you choose to run for more ammunition,*
  go to 76.
✢ *If you choose to fight the orochi with your staff,*
  go to 78.

54

"Yes, Shinigami!" you cry. "Powerful as you are – I challenge you!"

You loose off an arrow. The Lord of Death laughs contemptuously and turns it to ashes with a casual gesture. Then the demon reaches into the earth with its hand and pulls out a gigantic lump of flaming molten rock, which it hurls at you. You dodge, though it singes your hair and clothes as it passes. Then you shoot another arrow. You know you cannot defeat the demon, but if you can buy enough time...

You shoot more arrows and dodge more fiery rocks, but Shinigami grows tired of this game. He reaches out towards you with one great, shadowy

hand. Instantly, you are paralysed: you cannot move a muscle. You close your eyes and await your fate.

But the night is suddenly ripped apart by blinding light. You open your eyes to see, speeding from East and West, two great, glowing, wingless dragons – Kirin and Ryu, guardians of mankind.

Shinigami turns towards the dragons, and movement once again returns to your body.

‡ *If you wish to leave the dragons to deal with Shinigami, go to 33.*

‡ *If you wish to help the dragons in their fight with Shinigami, go to 100.*

55

More demons pour from the pit. Hatred of the living burns in their crimson eyes. The demons lift you off your feet and carry you down the smoking slope of the pit, mocking your cries for mercy as they haul you into its depths, tearing at your flesh as they go.

The earth rumbles once again. The demons screech as the cleft in the rocks begins to close. As the last of the light fades you know that, though they will once again be trapped underground, the demons have managed to bring with them something they greatly value: *you*. Tormenting humans is a demon's chief delight, and there are thousands of demons all around you thinking up evil and horrific torments for you.

‡ *Your hunt is over. If you want to begin again, go to 1.*

56

You draw the katana sword and with a warlike cry, you slash at the stone head with all your might.

The blade shatters against the demon head. The specially forged tamahagane steel is as strong as human craftsmanship can make it, but it is not designed to penetrate solid stone. Metal pieces fall to the floor and glow briefly as the magical kanji on the blade are destroyed before they can act on the demon. Your attack has failed. The head is unharmed, and you have lost your sword.

Before you react, the demon head attacks.

‡ *Go to 93.*

57

You scramble up onto the main cable and begin to climb. The demons rage and howl as they see you pass beyond their reach.

But the bridge was severely damaged during the earthquake, and the suspender cables joining the main cable continue to snap.

The main cable bucks and twangs beneath you, making it almost impossible to maintain your grip. You look over your shoulder and see some of the demons climbing up after you.

Finally, the main cable itself snaps. The bridge deck collapses with a roar, casting deck plates, girders and cars into the water.

The cable lashes like a whip, hurling you off the bridge and into the air. Helplessly, you too tumble towards the dark water of the bay.

‡ *Go to 95.*

58

You use your kama sickle to slash at the centipede. The scythe blade slices the creature's jointed body in half. You wait for it to turn to dust, as all the other demons you have defeated have done.

But instead, the two halves of the creature scuttle back together and join like sections of a vacuum-cleaner hose. You realise you are in more trouble than you thought.

> ‡ *To shoot the centipede with arrows, go to 41.*
> ‡ *To swim the river to the island, go to 49.*
> ‡ *To seek shelter in the temple, go to 22.*

59

You head for the zoo gates.

A demon tiger leaps out of the darkness, blocking your path. It has swollen to the size of a buffalo. Its face is set into a snarl of hatred: its golden stripes seem to burn against the darkness.

You raise your gun. "Hello, Kitty."

The tiger roars and springs away. You chase it. It is soon out of sight, but you continue to stalk it, like the hunter that you are. It cannot escape while you are on its trail.

The tiger seems to realise this. As you pass a clump of bushes, you hear a rustle to your right. You barely

have time to react as the maddened beast hurls itself
at you.

‡ *If you want to shoot it with rock salt, go to 91.*
‡ *If you choose to attack with the ninjato swords,
go to 65.*

60

You allow the call to connect, and Master Shoki's face
appears on the screen. Your tutor's face is impassive
as always, but a nerve twitches in his cheek. You can
tell he is worried. "Have you had an earthquake in
Okinawa?"

"Yes, and it released some interesting characters."
You tell Master Shoki about the opening of the
pit and your struggles with its demons. As you are
speaking, another earthquake strikes. You stagger, but
keep your feet and watch as the rift in the hillside
closes, sealing the underworld. "The pit has closed
again," you tell Master Shoki. "I can't see any more
demons – it looks like the danger is over."

"You are mistaken." Master Shoki's voice is sharp.
"The earthquake did not occur in Okinawa only. Here
in Tokyo, we felt it, too. And here also, portals have
opened into the underworld: I think more than one.
There are reports of demon activity from all over the
city. We need you here."

"I'm on my way," you tell the old demon hunter.

Soon you are in your helicopter and you fly towards the capital at maximum speed.

Darkness has fallen by the time you land on the helipad of a downtown office block. Master Shoki meets you on the roof. He is old and frail and has to use a walking stick. You know that his days of fighting demons have passed and you will have to face them on your own.

Master Shoki leads you down to the street where a powerful SUV is waiting. "A large group of demons is gathered around the giant Ferris wheel on Odaiba Island," he tells you. "I have preset your destination in the sat-nav." He holds out his hand. "Good luck."

You drive the powerful car through the crowded streets before crossing the Rainbow Bridge, with the dark waters of Tokyo bay far below. After a short drive you reach your destination. You open the back door of the vehicle and find that Master Shoki has packed every weapon you are ever likely to need. But you know that you cannot carry too much: you need agility as well as firepower to combat demons.

You select a shotgun and three ammunition belts. One contains standard cartridges; the second, rock salt, which is fatal to demons; and the third, dragon's breath cartridges which convert the shotgun into a flamethrower.

You now have a hand free to take one more weapon – but which?

Some shuriken throwing stars, which can magically trap demons.

A katana long sword, good for keeping enemies at a safe distance.

A deer-horn knife, ideal for close-quarter fighting.

‡ *To choose the shuriken throwing stars, go to 8.*
‡ *To choose the katana long sword, go to 51.*
‡ *To choose the deer-horn knife, go to 21.*

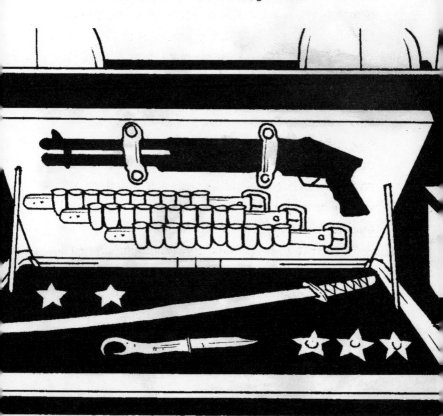

61

You climb to the top of the grass slope. Before you, a cliff leads to a hilltop. To your left, a river flows either side of a small island covered with trees. Smoke rises from the centre of the island, as though someone has built a fire there. To your right stands a torii gateway to a temple.

You hear a harsh screaming and a beating of wings in the air above you. You look up – and a flock of shikome demons, savage bird-shaped creatures with sharp talons and loathsome female heads, dive to the attack.

‡ *To battle the shikome, go to 7.*
‡ *If you wish climb the cliff, heading for the hilltop, go to 29.*
‡ *To stand with your back to the cliff, go to 92.*
‡ *To swim the river to the island, go to 49.*

62

"Demon," you say wearily, "I've heard enough from you."

The demon snarls. "I will not be silenced!"

You shrug. "On your own head be it."

You draw your sickle and swing it with all your might, but as you loosen your two-handed grip, the head wriggles free and instead of burying the blade in the demon's head, the sharp point plunges into your thigh. The kanji symbols do not blaze as they are spells to defeat demons, but blood spurts from the wound. You curse loudly as the demons regather themselves and take this opportunity to attack.

As the head flies around you, the other creatures move forward as one. You try to hold them off, but it is hopeless – they are too many of them for you to fight.

They overwhelm you and you crash down onto the carriage roof. Your weapon spins out of your hand and flies through the air out of sight.

‡ *Go to 88.*

63

You turn round to reach into the back of the SUV and grab the first weapon that comes to hand – a nunchaku rice flail. You wrench open the door. You are half-blinded by the spray of the crashing waves below. Debris falls from the disintegrating bridge like a hail of iron and steel, and broken cables whip across the roadway with a force sufficient to cut you in half.

You head for the nearest demons, and use the flail to clear a way through. Their unearthly flesh cannot withstand the touch of the kanji spells on the handles and each link of the chain that joins them. But though you destroy several demons, causing the rest to fall back, you quickly realise that you have only won yourself a brief respite. With every passing second, more demons are climbing onto the bridge. There are too many of them to fight with a single weapon. Your only hope is to escape.

‡ *If you decide to climb out of the demons' reach, go to 57.*

‡ *If you want to jump from the bridge and swim to safety, go to 95.*

64

Leaving the demons behind, you race up the hill towards your helicopter to pick up your weapons.

But when you reach the smoking hilltop, you find a very different landscape to the one you expected. Smoke belches out of a huge pit, which is full of strange shapes and eye-wrenching colours. The bottom of the crater is lost in thick, grey clouds. The air is full of strange and unearthly cries. Howls and screams of rage cause you to shudder with fear.

The acrid fumes make you cough. "Boy," you mutter, "this place really is the pits."

You move carefully round the edge of the fissure, your eyes streaming from the acrid smoke. You finally reach the helicopter. What should you do next?

‡ *If you wish to fly the helicopter back to the sumo ring, go to 23.*

‡ *If you wish to take the weapons pack from the helicopter and return to the stadium to fight the demons, go to 85.*

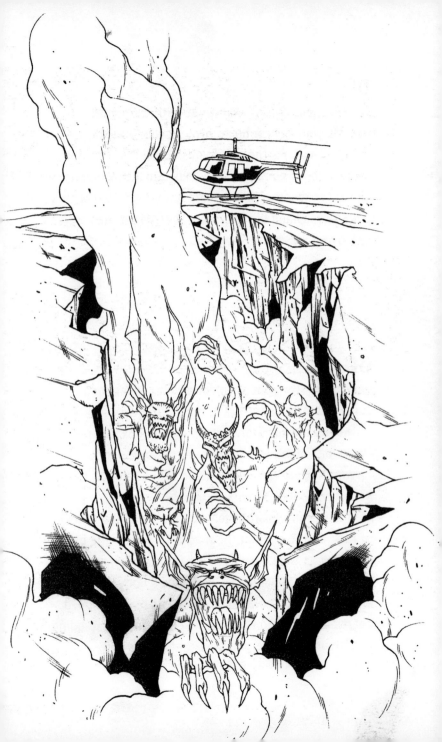

65

As the tiger charges, you lunge with the ninjato swords. But to your horror, you realise that they are too short. As the great cat impales itself on the swords and the magically inscribed blades pierce its heart, the dying creature tears out your throat with a huge paw. Blood bubbles from severed arteries as you fall, dying, beside the beast you have killed.

> ⸸ *Your hunt is over. If you wish to begin again, go to 1.*

66

You reach over your shoulder and draw the long, curved katana sword from its sheath on your back.

The demon turns and snarls at you, but you take the sword's long grip in both hands and lunge forward. The single-edged blade slides through the demon's bloated body.

The demon's snarl becomes a high-pitched squeal of rage and fear. Then the magical kanji on the blade glow red as they burn and tear into the demonic flesh. Smoke pours from the demon's body. It thrashes around, but you hold on grimly as its body is ripped apart by the sword's powerful spells, finally exploding in a cloud of smoke and dust that covers you.

You look up and see more demons readying themselves for an attack.

- ⸔ *If you think you need to get more weapons, go to 76.*
- ⸔ *If you want to carry on fighting the demons, go to 89.*

67

"Who are you?" you cry. "You look like Hashuk, but where is your bird? You are a demon imposter!"

You shoot at the dark-haired figure, but she moves with incredible speed and the arrow misses. She laughs, and throws back her hair revealing her nightmare face – red-eyed, cruel and mocking.

She gives a terrifying laugh. "No, I am not Hashuk. I am Kanesh, and I will drain the life from your body!"

She rushes towards you, dodging as you shoot more arrows. Before you can switch weapons, her hands tighten on your throat. Desperately you try to break free of her grip, but she has supernatural strength.

Her mouth opens, revealing rows of deadly sharp fangs, which she plunges into your flesh. Before you can cry out your blood is sucked from your body. You collapse to the floor, bloodless and lifeless.

- ⸔ *You have failed. If you wish to try again, go to 1.*

68

You return to your SUV and set off in pursuit of the bullet train.

But your progress through the city is very slow. The streets are still full of frightened crowds and abandoned vehicles. At last you reach an expressway and your progress is better – but before long, you arrive at the scene of a multi-vehicle crash. The road is completely blocked.

The police are at the scene. You approach a senior officer and explain your mission. He stares at you.

"Are you crazy?" he demands in Japanese. "It will take hours to clear the roads – and even if we could do it faster, how could you hope to catch the world's fastest train by chasing it in a car anyway?"

Unearthly lights fill the sky. Ominous clouds gather, glowing orange and purple. Lightning flashes from horizon to horizon, and the ground rocks as escaped demons open more portals to the underworld. In the distance fires spring up, explosions devastate the land as demons retake the living world from humankind.

Your heart is heavy – you realise that you are watching the beginning of the end of the world.

‡ *You have failed. If you want to begin again in your attempt to stop the demons destroying mankind, go to 1.*

69

You decide that there will be plenty of time to talk to Master Shoki once you have dealt with the situation here. You block his call and head to the pit.

You reach the edge of the smoking crater and begin to descend. All seems quiet.

But suddenly, the earth rumbles again, shaking beneath your feet. You guess this is an aftershock from the earthquake that let the demons out into the world. You lose your balance and fall to your knees. You watch horrified as hundreds of demons of all shapes and sizes begin pouring out of the smoking pit, heading towards you. You deliver a series of martial arts moves that cause the demons to back off. However, you soon realise that there are too many of them to fight – you are in a terrible situation.

‡ *If you wish to surrender and throw yourself on their mercy, go to 55.*
‡ *If you want to try and escape, go to 42.*

70

You chase after the stone head. This is difficult as it keeps bouncing off in random directions, and you cannot predict where it will go next. You shoot at the demon, but it easily avoids you. All the time, its toll of victims is increasing.

You sprint hard and succeed in catching up with the head. It seems to realise that you are an enemy. It bounces on the spot, glaring at you with its staring eyes, and snarling defiance.

"You are one ugly beast," you growl. "You wouldn't like yourself in a mirror."

"Hunterrr," it rumbles in a voice like a rockslide, "you werrre foolish to come herrre!"

Before you can answer, the head gives a howl of demonic rage and hurls itself into the attack.

   ‡ *To shoot the head with rock salt, go to 4.*
   ‡ *To shoot the head with dragon's breath cartridges, go to 37.*
   ‡ *To attack the head with your katana sword, go to 56.*

71

You use your hanbo staff to fight off the demon bear. It roars with rage and swipes at you with its deadly paws, but you are an expert with this weapon. The kanji spells inscribed on the ash wood are a torment to the demon possessing the bear's body. Every time you score a hit on its body, the kanji symbols burn its fur. You move in, smashing the creature with the quarterstaff, keeping well clear of its claws. You land a series of blows and the kanji take effect. The bear suddenly glows red. You stand back and watch as the demon within the creature is destroyed.

The bear immediately shrinks to its normal size. It shakes its head as though surrounded by bees. Then, confused, it hobbles away, whining.

You move away from the bear and head towards the other demons that are on the loose. A bloated spider with a woman's face, is hanging from the roof of a kiosk. There is a troop of demon baboons wrecking the gift shop and you also spot an orochi, an eight-headed dragon, heading out of the park gates, no doubt intent on causing death and destruction on the streets of Tokyo.

- ⚵ *If you decide to tackle the spider-woman, go to 28.*
- ⚵ *If you wish to attack the baboons, go to 40.*
- ⚵ *If you choose to tackle the orochi, go to 83.*

72

"Thank you, honourable shi-shi," you say, "but I fear your strength may not be enough to overcome Shinigami, Lord of Death. Could you instead act as messengers to summon more powerful aid?"

The shi-shi exchange glances. "Yes, we can," says the first. "We will summon the dragon Kirin..."

"And the dragon Ryn," adds the second.

Remembering your fight with the orochi, you shudder. "I do not ask you to summon demons."

The shi-shi roar angrily. "Kirin and Ryn are no demons! They are guardians of humanity."

You bow low. "In that case, thank you. Please ask for their aid – and run like the wind as time is short!"

The shi-shi race away as you set off again, up the mountain. You know you cannot hope to defeat the great lord of the demons, but maybe you can distract him until help arrives.

But your courage begins to fail as, blinded by mists and buffeted by storms, you reach the summit of the sacred mountain, and find yourself facing Shinigami.

The Lord of Death wears a jet-black robe, gathered around the waist with a belt of human skulls. He has the head of a savage ape surrounded by a mane of spiky black hair, bound in a headband fashioned from a shroud. Vast, bat-like wings rise from his shoulders, and he carries a scythe.

The most terrible of demons stares down at you, its ape-like face twisted in an expression of cruel mockery. "Pathetic mortal!" it cries. "Do you presume to challenge me?"

You know you have to try and play for time until the dragons arrive. But which is the best way to do it?

‡ *If you wish to beg for mercy, go to 84.*
‡ *If you want to attack Shinigami, go to 54.*

73

You recall what Master Shoki told you about ashin demons. These are creatures that exist in pairs. Each demon possesses a bodily feature that acts in harmony with a feature of the other.

Master Shoki's words come back to you: "Hunter-san, one demon of a pair may have huge eyes, and be able to see across great distances: while the other will have great ears, and be able to hear the quietest of whispers. By themselves, these demons are very dangerous: but if they are threatened, they join together, and their power becomes ten times greater."

You realise that Long-arms and Long-legs are ashin demons, and if you are to have any chance of defeating them, you must keep them apart.

‡ *If you decide you will need more weapons, go to 64.*
‡ *To fight both ashin at the same time, go to 30.*
‡ *If you want to try and keep the ashin apart, go to 19.*

74

The figure leads you back into the forest. You continue to descend and eventually find yourself wading through stinking mud surrounded by the white skeletons of dead trees.

"Hashuk!" you cry. "Why are you leading me away from the mountain?" The figure makes no reply: she leaps from hummock to hummock of springy grass, somehow avoiding the dank waters of the swamp.

‡ *To continue to follow the figure, go to 18.*
‡ *To leave her and go on alone, go to 46.*
‡ *To shoot an arrow at the figure, go to 67.*

75

You return to your SUV and head across the Rainbow
Bridge towards the office where you met Master Shoki.

But as you begin to cross the bridge, another
aftershock strikes. The roadway trembles, brakes
screech and traffic comes to a halt. Frightened drivers
and their passengers stare around wildly.

You hear a series of snaps, like the cracking of
huge whips. Cables break and the roadway tilts. Giant
waves rise up from the bay – there are water demons
riding them! They land on the bridge and clamber over
the abandoned cars.

‡ *To swing the car around and turn back, go to 35.*
‡ *To stop the car and wait for the chaos to subside,
   go to 87.*
‡ *If you want to try to escape on foot, go to 63.*

76

You race towards your vehicle to retrieve more weapons and ammunition, but the pursuing demons are faster. Long fingers clutch at your clothing. Long legs stretch out to trip you. Bat-like wings flap in your face, blinding you.

You stumble and fall. Immediately, the demon swarm is upon you.

"Hunterrrrr," they hiss, "you have killed ssssso many of our breed, ssssso many! Now, you will pay!"

You scream as they set about eating you alive.

✝ *Your hunt is over. If you wish to begin again, go to 1.*

77

You swing the kama sickle. Its curved blade cleaves through undead flesh. But you cannot kill creatures that are already dead.

The demons snarl with hate. "You are a fool, Hunterrr," they cry, "you cannot harm us!"

"Maybe not," you say, "but I can make you harmless..." You swing the sickle twice. "...by making you arm-less." A goryo stares at the two undead arms which your weapon has severed from its shoulders and which now lie, twitching, on the carriage roof.

The goryo stares as you aim a karate kick at its chest: a split second later, it tumbles from the train.

You whirl around, spinning from foot to foot until the blade of your sickle is no more that a shimmering arc of light. You chop at the demons' limbs, cleaving them from their bodies. The surviving demons draw away from you. But just as you think you have won the battle, the carriage roof below your feet explodes outwards, and new foe emerges – a nukekubi demon.

You know that this demon is a fearsome opponent. You barely have time to react as the demon reaches up and tears its head from its shoulders. Eyes flashing with hatred, deadly jaws agape and ready to bite, crush and devour, the head leaps from the demon's grasp and flies to the attack!

‡ *To block the attack with the tonfa club,*
  go to 82.
‡ *To attack the head with your sickle,*
  go to 14.
‡ *To shoot the nukebuki's body with an arrow,*
  go to 39.

78

You reach for your hanbo staff and launch into a furious attack. Spinning and leaping with lightning speed, you manage to land several blows with the staff. The kanji spells blaze brightly and cause the demon to howl in pain and rage.

But the orochi, though in pain is too big and powerful to succumb to being beaten. It fights back with its powerful claws, and before long your staff is smashed to pieces.

As the demon snaps at you with its nearest head, you hurl the shattered fragments of the staff into its gaping mouth.

The surprised beast gulps, and swallows. The ash wood, which had little effect on the dragon's hide, is more deadly inside the demon, as are the kanji spells carved into it. The orochi swells like a balloon – and explodes into vapour.

The remaining animal demons wail and leave their victims. Terrified animals rush off into the night. Recapturing all the creatures from the zoo will be a major headache – but, thankfully, someone else's. Your business is with demons, and by destroying the orochi you have stopped the threat from this nest.

‡ *Go to 24.*

79

You turn round to see Long-legs and Long-arms charging towards you, and open the fan with a flick of your wrist.

The demons are startled by the sudden movement, and hesitate. Your heart is beating wildly: you know you will only have one chance to defeat these demons; there is only one way in which such a seemingly frail weapon can work against them.

So you force yourself to appear calm. Standing facing the demons, you signal towards them.

"Come and get me, then, if you think you can..."

Your mockery enrages the demons – exactly as you planned. They try to join together to increase their strength.

But they have fallen into your trap and you are ready. Just as Long-arms leaps onto Long-legs's shoulders, you skim the fan, like a Frisbee, so that it slices between the twin demons.

They cannot join against the barrier of the fan. For a moment, they gaze at you in shock – then the magical kanji inscribed on the fan start to work and the demons explode into clouds of dust and smoke. With wails of despair, they disappear.

You grin. "That is one fan-tastic weapon."

You look around. All seems quiet. But you remember Master Shoki's words of warning during your training: "In any nest of demons, there are always a few more powerful than the rest. If you can defeat these chief demons, the others will also be destroyed."

You also know from your research into demons that they can be tricky and sly. If even one demon escapes destruction, it can cause untold chaos. It might even find a way to reopen the portal by which it came into the world, and clear the way for others.

You know that you may not have destroyed all the demons. You will have to check the pit on the hill – there is still smoke rising from it. Your smartphone rings. You check the screen. It is Master Shoki.

‡ *If you want to check the pit first, go to 69.*
‡ *If you decide to take the call, go to 60.*

80

Shinigami wears a jet-black robe, gathered around the
waist with a belt of human skulls. He has the head
of a savage ape surrounded by a mane of spiky black
hair, bound in a headband fashioned from a shroud.
Vast, bat-like wings rise from his shoulders, and he
carries a scythe.

The death-demon laughs, in a voice that causes
avalanches to rumble away down the mountain.
"Foolish mortal! Do you seek to challenge my power?"

In answer, you raise your bow and shoot – but
Shinigami burns the arrow to ashes in mid-air with
a casual gesture. The death-demon gestures again,
and your other weapons fly away to be lost in the
night. You turn to run but Shinigami reaches out with
a shadowy hand – and you feel the blood boiling in
your veins and your flesh dissolving.

Even as your life is slipping away, you see the death-demon raise a clenched fist into the air, and as the volcano spews forth fire, demons of all shapes, colours and sizes pour out. You watch helplessly as thousands of the supernatural creatures fly through the air and scuttle down the mountain, heading off to destroy mankind and conquer the world.

Shinigami the Lord of Death, turns his attention back to you. With a gesture of his hand, a powerful and invisible force picks you up and casts you screaming into the fiery pit below.

Even after all your struggles, your hunt is over.

‡ *If you have the true heart of a Hunter, and wish to begin again, go to 1.*

81

You race to the bottom of the Ferris wheel and look up. The hibagon is still climbing. The demons that have been swarming all over the wheel make way for it, hissing with respect. The creature uses its long arms, powerful hands and ape-like feet to grip the stays and girders of the wheel.

"King Kong was a pussycat compared to this thing," you mutter to yourself. The hibagon shows no sign of pausing in its climb, and the child it has taken is still screaming for its parents, who stand wailing and wringing their hands.

- ‡ *If you decide to shoot the hibagon, go to 11.*
- ‡ *If you want to climb the wheel and attack the demon with your sword, go to 12.*

82

You block the head's attack by using the tonfa club as an armshield.

But while the head distracts you, flying in to the attack but always turning aside at the last moment to evade your wild swings, other undead demons creep up behind. A horde of the foul creatures pounces, overwhelming you. They pull at your legs and cause you to overbalance. You crash onto the carriage roof, winded. Your weapons slip from your grasp and spin off into the air. The nukekubi's head returns to its shoulders, and the creature gloats as more demons move in for the kill.

- ‡ *Go to 6.*

83

You decide that the orochi dragon is your most pressing target. It is the biggest, and capable of causing most destruction. You also know that it is likely to be the leader of this nest and if you can defeat it, the other demons in this horde will be destroyed.

Even so, it is a formidable opponent. You grit your teeth. "The bigger they are, the harder they fall," you tell yourself. Hoping that this old saying is true, you race after the orochi.

It senses your approach. Eight gigantic heads swing round towards you. The fearsome beast rears up, and you change direction just in time to avoid eight searing gouts of flame from its gaping jaws.

You wipe the sweat from your brow. "That's what I call a warm welcome," you mutter.

You consider your next move. Dragon's breath cartridges will clearly not work against a monster that breathes fire. That leaves the rock-salt cartridges, and the hanbo quarterstaff.

‡ *If you wish to shoot the demon with rock salt, go to 53.*

‡ *If you choose to fight with the staff, go to 78.*

84

"Spare me, O great Shinigami!" you cry.

The Lord of Death laughs, causing the mountain to shake and avalanches to thunder down its slopes. "Foolish wretch! Demons show no mercy!"

He gestures at you with his hand and your body is gripped by powerful demonic force. You cannot move!

Shinigami raises a clenched fist to the sky. The crater of the volcano at his feet bursts open. Flames leap high into the air, and the Lord of Death's demon followers stream out. "Feed on him," he commands.

Screeching with triumphant laughter, his minions rip the flesh from your body until you are nothing more than a pile of white bones.

‡ *You have fallen at the final hurdle. If you have the heart of a Hunter and wish to begin again, go to 1.*

85

You open the helicopter's cargo door, and pull out the case containing your new martial arts weapons.

Inside there are a number of devices designed to banish the creatures of the underworld including:

A pair of sui three-bladed, close-fighting daggers;

A mankiri, a throwing weapon, consisting of a chain with weights on the end;

A Korean fighting fan.

These weapons are made of rare materials and exotic metal alloys. They are all inscribed with powerful kanji, picture-like symbols. These kanji contain spells to destroy or banish demons.

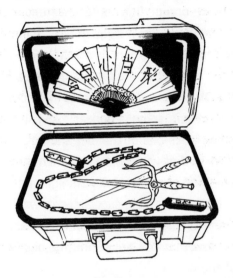

As you hesitate, undecided as to which weapon to take, you sense movement behind you. You spin around – it is Long-legs and Long-arms!

You have a split second to make your choice, and time to snatch only one weapon.

‡ *To take the sui daggers, go to 94.*
‡ *To take the mankiri chain weapon, go to 38.*
‡ *To take the Korean fighting fan, go to 79.*

86

You hear a terrible roar, the distant sound of many demon voices raised in triumph. You look up, towards the peak of Mount Fuji.

The snowy upper slopes of the sacred mountain are bathed in weird orange light reflected from roiling, lightning-flecked clouds. A huge gout of flame rises from the volcano. Lava pours down the snow-covered slopes: where it touches, ice flashes into steam.

And through the clouds of vapour, the monstrous shapes of mountain demons appear: hawk-like tengu; Raijin and Raiji, demons of thunder and lightning, Fujin, demon-lord of wind and his followers, harpy-like shikome; and greatest of all, Shinigami, the Lord of Death. The demons have succeeded in waking the mountain and the doors of the underworld are open wide. You know that you are seeing the beginning of the end of the world.

‡ *You have failed to save humankind. If you want to try again, go to 1.*

87

You sit tight as waves wash over the bridge and water lashes at your car, causing the engine to cut out. You see to your horror that huge numbers of water

86
87

demons are climbing over the barriers at either side of the roadway. Drivers and passengers from stranded cars take one look at the horrors, scream and flee.

You turn your head to look out of the side and rear windows, and realise that there are demons all around you. There's something fishy going on here, you think.

You're right. These demons have taken on the shapes of various sea creatures, each more terrifying and loathsome than the last. There are tentacled sea demons like giant squid and octopus; frog-like kappa, with long legs and bulging eyes, agile and dangerous; gigantic eels and water-snakes; human-shaped demons with the heads of shark and barracuda. And all of them are heading for you!

‡ *If you wish to start the engine and use the car as a battering ram to escape, go to 25.*

‡ *If you want to abandon the car and try to escape on foot, go to 63.*

‡ *If you decide to jump from the bridge and swim to safety, go to 95.*

88

The undead demons seize you, laughing, and the train speeds up. As soon as it reaches its top speed of 180 miles per hour, they throw you off the carriage roof.

As you soar through the air, you try to restart the jet pack, but it fails to fire. You try to brace yourself for the impact: but it is useless. You hit the ground with stunning force: you feel bones break and internal organs burst. The train, with its load of jeering demons, speeds away.

> ‡ *You have failed to save the world from the demons. If you want to try again, go to 1.*

89

You look around for your next targets – they are not hard to find.

A blazing wheel, almost ten metres in diameter, is thundering towards you leaving a fiery trail in its wake. Screaming people scatter from its path. Balancing on top of the wheel, and turning it with her feet like a circus performer, is a demon woman who cackles madly as it pursues its terrified victims.

Elsewhere, a huge stone head is bounding around like a gigantic, self-propelled basketball. Its features are savage and grotesque. It bounces among the crowd, spitting: and every person touched by its demonic saliva instantly turns to stone.

Finally, you glance at the Ferris wheel, where a screaming human family is pointing upwards. You see that a gigantic, ape-like creature with shaggy orange fur has snatched a child. You recognise this demon as a hibagon, a creature similar to the Bigfoot of North America. Clutching the screaming child, it is climbing the Ferris wheel.

These are your targets, but which one do you wish to attack first?

‡ *To attack the demon wheel rider, go to 26.*
‡ *To attack the stone head demon, go to 70.*
‡ *To attack the hibagon, go to 81.*

90

"Honoured shi-shi," you say, bowing low, "please accept my apologies. I would not have disturbed your rest, or the peace of this holy place, but I had no choice." You explain your mission to the lion-guardians of the temple.

The shi-shi converse in low voices. Then they turn to you. "We accept your good faith, and the urgency of your mission," says one.

The other growls agreement. "We are only humble temple guardians, but we will try to assist you."

You are tired, running out of weapons, and sorely in need of help – but are these creatures really powerful enough to be of help when you challenge the greatest demon of all, Shinigami, Lord of Death?

‡ *To accept the shi-shis' offer of help, go to 16.*
‡ *If you choose to go on alone, and ask the shi-shi to summon more powerful assistance, go to 72.*

91

The shotgun blast is effective! The controlling demon screams as the rock salt enters the tiger's flesh, and leaves its victim. The tiger looks startled before it shrinks to its normal size. Then it drops down dead.

You realise that you made a mistake choosing

the short daggers – if the tiger had leapt at you, the daggers would not have worked – you need something to keep the animal demons at bay. You head back to the helicopter, pick up more ammunition and take the long, ash wood hanbo quarterstaff.

You head back into the park where there are still plenty of demons causing havoc. A bloated spider with a woman's face is hanging from a nearby tree, a troop of demon baboons is trashing a souvenir shop – and an orochi, an eight-headed dragon, is heading out of the park intent on causing yet more chaos.

‡ *If you decide to tackle the spider-woman, go to 28.*
‡ *If you wish to attack the baboons, go to 40.*
‡ *If you choose to tackle the orochi, go to 83.*

92

You back up against the cliff, and raise your bow. Now the shikome can only come at you from the front. You shoot several, while the others hang back.

"Bye bye, birdies," you taunt them.

As you notch another arrow to your bow, you stumble over the ribcage of a human skeleton. You stare around and realise that the ground beneath your feet is littered with grisly human remains.

At the same moment, you hear a horrible chittering noise behind you. You turn and give a gasp of horror. A giant centipede crawls out from a narrow cave in the rocks and stalks towards you on its multitude of legs, mandibles clacking. You recognise it as a flesh-eating omukade demon.

‡ *If you wish climb the cliff to escape, go to 29.*
‡ *To fight the giant centipede, go to 58.*
‡ *To jump into the river and swim to the islet, go to 49.*

93

Before you can move, the demon head spits at you. A glistening, green gobbet of demon saliva hits you in the chest. From the point of impact, numbness spreads through your body, solidifying your muscles, stopping the flow of blood in your veins as your body turns to stone.

Although you can no longer move, you are still able to see and hear. The demon has clearly not finished with you yet. It bounces high in the sky and comes down straight towards you. Your final conscious thought is one of sheer horror, as you realise that the demon intends to bounce on your rocky remains until it reduces you to pebbles, gravel, and finally, powder.

‡ *You have failed. If you still think you are hard enough to tangle with demons, go to 1.*

94

You spin around and drop into a fighting stance as Long-arms and Long-legs race to attack you.

You meet the attack bravely, but the sui daggers you have chosen are useless against this pair. They are not designed as throwing knives, and you cannot get close enough to the demons for them to be effective. Long-arms holds you at arm's length whilst Long-legs delivers devastating kicks, which knock the breath from your body and the daggers from your hands.

You are like a rag doll in a child's hands. You cannot break from Long-arms' tight grip.

The two demons join together and the grip tightens on you tenfold. The newly formed creature takes huge strides up the hillside towards the pit from where it came from. It takes the demon only a few seconds before it flings you to the ground. Through battered eyes you see dozens more demons of all shapes and sizes surrounding you. You struggle to your feet, fearful of what is going to happen.

"Please don't," you beg...

‡ Go to 55.

95

You plummet feet-first into the icy water of the bay. The shock of hitting the water from such a height causes agony to shoot through your whole body, almost knocking you out. You fight the pain and struggle to the surface. You break through the waves and gasp a great lungful of air. You have survived a drop from a tremendous height: you are alive!

But there are other things in the water with you: demons! You open your mouth to scream and it fills with salt water, choking you.

The demons attack, seizing you in their terrible jaws and dragging you down into the freezing water.

⚓ *Your hunt is over. If you want to begin again, go to 1.*

96

The dog demon leaps to the attack and you fend it off with your tonfa club. From the corner of your eyes you see Hashuk engage the icicle demon. Clearly you will get no help from her, and you soon realise that the dog demon is too strong for you. You have no hope in a fight at close quarters and, as the demon continues to press its attack, you have no time to draw your bow and set an arrow to the string.

The time has come for desperate measures. You fling your club over the dog's head. "Fetch!"

As you hoped, the creature's instincts take control and it leaps to catch the club in its snapping jaws.

Its momentary distraction is all the opportunity you need. You raise your bow and shoot an ash-wood arrow into the demon's exposed chest. The deadly shaft penetrates the creature's heart: it gives a whine of despair and dissolves into smoke.

"Good boy. Play dead," you mutter grimly.

You look around – but Hashuk and the icicle demon have disappeared.

Then a figure appears, lower down the slope – a woman with long dark hair. The figure beckons to you. You are not sure whether to follow. You look around – there is no sign of the goddess's hawk. The figure beckons again.

‡ *If you want to follow the figure, go to 74.*
‡ *If you choose to go on alone, go to 46.*

97

You continue to fight valiantly, but eventually you run out of arrows. The demons close in, tearing your weapons away. Cackling in triumph, the creatures knock you off your feet and grab hold of you. You try to struggle free, but you are firmly in their grip. The creatures take you to the hilltop where a hidden smoking pit gapes in the side of the mountain. You cry out knowing that this is the doorway to the underworld from which the demons have so recently escaped. You cry out in anguish, knowing full well that they are going to take you to the pit from which there will be no return for you.

‡ *Go to 55.*

98

You watch in horrified fascination as the woman's face contorts, quickly losing any resemblance to anything human. She is a demon! The man screams and tries to break away from the creature. But the demon has a grip of iron. Your stomach churns with revulsion as the skin of her face ripples, sags and folds into something foul and inhuman.

Before you can react, her dress seems to wrap itself around the struggling man, who screams in torment as, before your appalled gaze, his skin and bones dissolve like the body of a melting snowman and the hideous demon absorbs his flesh into her own unearthly substance. The demon turns her gaze towards you and emits a high piercing howl. Answering the call, more demons begin to head towards you.

‡ *If you think you need to get more weapons, go to 76.*
‡ *If you decide to shoot the demon woman, go to 44.*
‡ *If you choose to use your sword, go to 66.*

99

You choose the bow and arrows and secure them to your body. Then you step off the roof. For several seconds, you are in free-fall. Then the wind lifts your kite. As you level out, you fire up the jet pack. You feel as if a giant hand has grabbed you and flung you through the air. Master Shoki's jet kite works!

You shoot over the city, and then out across the dark countryside. You find the silver ribbon of the Kyoto railway line: then, far ahead you see the lights of the bullet train.

You increase speed. Soon you are racing alongside the train. The demons inside the carriages howl at you as you swoop over the train and land on the roof.

The carriage windows below you are smashed, and a horde of undead demons swarm onto the roof. They seem to be able to cling to any surface. Soon you are surrounded by goryo - zombie-like corpses reanimated by demons.

Balancing carefully on the roof of the train, you power down the jet kite and release the straps holding it to your back. The wind picks up the kite as you release it, blowing it high into the air where it disappears in the darkness.

You quickly loose off an arrow – the ash wood is deadly to demons, and the arrow shaft flies through three goryo zombies, reducing them to dust.

The remaining demons hesitate – but more windows are breaking all the way down the train and a ghastly army of troll-like oni, ghoulish moryo, nuri with blackened flesh and dangling eyeballs, living skeletons and flesh-eating goblins emerges, advancing on you. You reach for your arrows, but there are too many demons and you decide to switch weapons.

‡ *To use the tonfa club, go to 52.*
‡ *To use the kama sickle, go to 77.*

100

Shinigami bellows and folds his bat-wings over his eyes to keep out the blazing light. The dragons fly around the summit of the volcano, singing a wordless song. The crater opens, but not to release more demons. Instead, a spinning vortex appears. Violent wind whips up as the vortex rushes down the mountainside, sucking demons back into the pit.

Shinigami roars with anger and scoops handfuls of fire from the volcano to hurl at the dragons. Kirin and Ryu try to avoid the fireballs, and you realise that Shinigami is far from finished. You quickly draw your bow and notch an arrow.

With unerring accuracy, you send an ash-shafted arrow into the Lord of Death's heart. Shinigami turns on you. His ape face is drawn in a look of horror as the kanji work their magic. The demon staggers back to the edge of the pit. You loose off another arrow, again hitting the demon smack in the chest.

Shinigami tumbles helplessly into the fiery pit. The earth roars and the crater reseals itself, then there is silence. The light fades from the sky, and with it the dragons Kirin and Ryu. You bow deeply in thanks.

Then, once more, light appears in the east.

It is the dawn – a new day begins.

You fall to your knees. The demons are vanquished, and the Earth is saved.

This time you have beaten the forces of the supernatural, but you know that more creatures are simply waiting, biding their time. At some time in the future, they will appear – and you will be ready...

Weapons armoury

The Hunter has a deadly range of weapons available
for each mission. In *Demon Hunter* these include
not only modern high-tech gear, but also ancient,
mystical weapons specially crafted to combat demons
from the underworld.

1. A Korean fighting fan might sound like a load of rubbish,
but it can be thrown and is inscribed with magical kanji.

2. A mankiri is a powerful chain throwing weapon, which
can wrap around opponents. The only problem is, if they're
still alive you'll have to go to get it back.

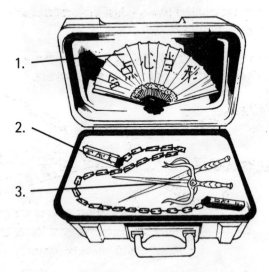

3. Sui three-bladed daggers are perfect for fighting up
close, but how close do you want to get? They also
can't be thrown.

4. The shotgun can be loaded with different types of ammunition, making it very versatile. These must be used against the right opponents though!

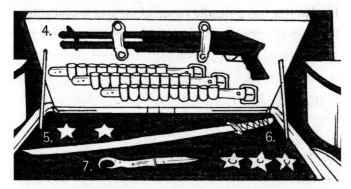

5. Shuriken stars can trap demons from a distance, but you don't have many of them.

6. A katana long sword is a very potent weapon, especially when it has magical powers. Just be careful which opponents it is used against.

7. A deer-horn knife is great at fighting close up, but it's a weapon that might have limited use.

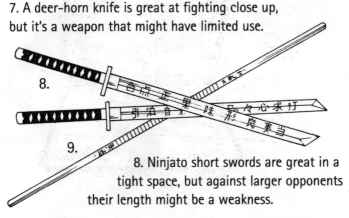

8. Ninjato short swords are great in a tight space, but against larger opponents their length might be a weakness.

9. Ash is deadly to some demons, so this hanbo quarterstaff could come in handy. But it isn't a blade weapon, so it can't cut like a sword.

Creating the artwork of iHorror

The inside artwork for iHorror is drawn by Paul Davidson. We've put together some pieces to show you the stages of progression. Below is the scene from paragraph 1, when the first demons emerge. Paul says: "We've merged the rough pencil and ink final alongside each other below. I do a pencil sketch to get the positions – I can do this quite quickly. This is then approved before I finish off each piece in black ink."

"The icicle demon really stands out against the black background."

⑨

"Here the art format changed completely, from portrait to landscape. I brought some of the flying demons closer for added impact."

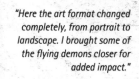

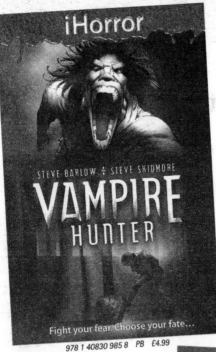

iHorror

STEVE BARLOW + STEVE SKIDMORE

VAMPIRE HUNTER

Fight your fear. Choose your fate...

978 1 40830 985 8   PB   £4.99

Tonight you've tracked a vampire to its underground hiding place in the city. It's cold – snow is falling – and in the dark a distant power is stirring ...

Load your weapons. Prime your senses. It's time!

You're called to an island in the South Pacific – home to the Nutco Oil corporation. Their operation is being disrupted by the sort of pest that only you can help to defeat – zombies!

They are threatening to destroy everything on the island of Saruba, and now you must fight your way through the fog and hordes of living dead to find the truth...

iHorror

STEVE BARLOW + STEVE SKIDMORE

ZOMBIE HUNTER

Fight your fear. Choose your fate...

978 1 40830 986 5   PB   £4.99

iHorror

Win a Nintendo DS Lite!*

The hunt is on...

Prove your skill as a hunter by locating the Hunter silhouettes lurking in the pages of the iHorror books (your first one is at the bottom of this page). Once you have found them in ALL FOUR iHorror titles, write the TOTAL number of silhouettes on a postcard with your name, age and address, and send it to:

iHorror Hunter Competition
Orchard Books Marketing Department
338 Euston Road
London NW1 3BH

Or email your answer and details to:
competitions@hachettechildrens.co.uk

Competition closes 31 August 2011.

For full terms and conditions visit:
www.orchardbooks.co.uk

Fight your fear. Choose your fate.

*This competition will run across all four iHorror books published in 2011. There will be one prize draw. Only one entry per child.

ANTHONY
HOROWITZ
GRAPHIC HORROR

An instant hit of horror from best-selling author, Anthony Horowitz. Scare yourself silly with these four haunting graphic novels:

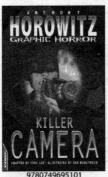

9780749695101

9780749695118

9780749695125

9780749695095

OUT NOW!

www.franklinwatts.co.uk.